Time for School, Little Blue Truck

Alice Schertle

Illustrated in the style of
Jill McElmurry
by John Joseph

Clarion Books
An Imprint of HarperCollinsPublishers
Boston   New York

Horn went "**Beep!**"
Engine purred.
Friendliest sounds
you ever heard.

Little Blue Truck
came down the road
early one morning
with good friend Toad.

Little Blue Truck called,
"Beep! Beep! Hi!"
to a big, bright school bus
passing by.

What a wonderful bus,
all shiny and yellow!
She stopped and smiled.
"Hi, little fellow!"

Inside, everyone sat in a row.
They waved out the windows to Blue below.

Little Duck called, "**Quack!**"
"There's school today!"
Little Goat said, "**Maaa!**"
Little Horse said, "**Neigh!**"

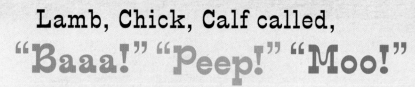

Lamb, Chick, Calf called,
"Baaa!" "Peep!" "Moo!"
"We're taking the bus
to school, Little Blue!"

"What a wonderful job!"
said Little Blue.
"I wish I were
a school bus too."

"You're a good little truck," the school bus said.
"But this job needs a *bus* instead!

I'm shiny yellow!
I'm long and wide
with lots of windows—
and seats inside!"

As the bus drove off
Blue heard her say,
"Mustn't be late
for school today!"

Down the road went Little Blue,
still wishing he were a school bus too.

They were almost home
when Blue said, "Toad!
That's Piggy crying—
by the road!"

"**Oink! Oink!** I'm late!"
poor Piggy wept.
"I missed the bus!
I overslept!"

"**Beep! Beep!** Don't cry,"
said Little Blue.
"Climb in. Let's see
what I can do.

"By now the bus is way ahead.
We'll take another way instead."

Blue made a turn
and left the road.
"Hang on, Piggy!
Hang on, Toad!

"I know a path
right through this wood.
I'll get you there
like a school bus should."

Bump! Bump! Bump!

The path was rough,
and Blue was little.
But Blue was tough.

There were bushes and brambles and towering trees.
"**Croak!**" said Toad. "It's quite a squeeze—
there's no room here for a great big bus!"

"**Beep!**" said Blue. "There's room for us!"

"**Who?**" called an owl
with mild surprise,
and looked at Blue
with big round eyes.

A gray squirrel chattered,
"**Chee! Chee! Chee!**"
and jumped along
from tree to tree.

When they came to a stream,
Blue splashed right in.
"**Beep! Beep!**" he said
with a little blue grin.

"I'm good at streams
and getting wet.
A little water
never stopped me yet!"

Through the woods—
what a bumpy ride!

Then . . .
there was the road
on the other side.

"**Oink!**" yelled Piggy.
"You did it, Blue!
I see the school,
and the school bus too!"

"**Beep!**" said Blue.
"It wasn't hard."
And he drove right into
the school bus yard.

The school bus stared
and blinked her eyes.
"Looks like this job
is just your size!

"You're not big, not yellow,
not long and wide,
but you had room
for a friend inside."

"You did this job in your very own way.
We needed a tough little truck today!"

Neigh! Peep! Oink!
Quack! Baaa! Moo!

Everybody cheered,
"GOOD JOB, BLUE!"

To Jen, Drew, Spence, Dylan, Kate, John, Marrie, and Aaron — A.S.

For all of my students, who light up the world in their very own way — J.J.

Text copyright © 2021 by Alice Schertle
Illustrations copyright © 2021 by The Estate of Jill McElmurry
Illustrated in the style of Jill McElmurry by John Joseph

clarionbooks.com/littlebluetruck

Design by Phil Caminiti

Library of Congress Cataloging-in-Publication Data is on file.

ISBN: 978-0-358-41224-3

Manufactured in China
SCP 15 14 13 12 11 10 9 8 7